Houndsley
and
Catina
at the Library

Houndsley
and
Catina
at the Library

James Howe

illustrated by Marie-Louise Gay

CANDLEWICK PRESS

In memory of Winifred Genung,
my first librarian—
and to all librarians, past, present, and future.
Where would we be without you?
J. H.

To Nakoa
M.-L. G.

Text copyright © 2020 by James Howe
Illustrations copyright © 2020 by Marie-Louise Gay

Candlewick Sparks®. Candlewick Sparks
is a registered trademark of Candlewick Press, Inc.

First paperback edition 2022

Library of Congress Catalog Card Number 2020900908
ISBN 978-0-7636-9662-7 (hardcover)
ISBN 978-1-5362-2359-0 (paperback)

22 23 24 25 26 27 CCP 10 9 8 7 6 5 4 3 2 1

Printed in Shenzhen, Guangdong, China

This book was typeset in Galliard and Tree-Boxelder.
The illustrations were done in watercolor, pencil, and collage.

Candlewick Press
99 Dover Street
Somerville, Massachusetts 02144

www.candlewick.com

Contents

Chapter One
Saturday Mornings

"Are you ready?" Bert asked his neighbor Houndsley.

"I will be, just as soon as I take my muffins out of the oven," Houndsley said.

"Oh, muffins!" Bert cried. "What kind are they?"

"Whole-wheat banana walnut. When we come back from the library, we will have some with tea."

"Yum," said Bert.

Bert loved Houndsley's muffins. Bert loved everything Houndsley made. Houndsley was a good cook. And Bert was a good eater.

"I'm ready," said Houndsley. "Next stop, Catina's house!"

"Hooray!" Bert said.

It was Saturday morning. Every Saturday morning, the three friends went to the library together. Then they came back to Houndsley's house to have tea and some of Houndsley's delicious muffins. They looked forward to their Saturday mornings all week.

"Good morning!" Catina called out from her front door.

"Good morning!" Houndsley and Bert called back.

At the library, they said hello to Trixie.

Trixie had been the librarian for as long as

they could remember. She always greeted

them with a smile, a new joke, and a book

to recommend.

But today she didn't smile when she said hello. When they asked her if she had heard any new jokes, she shook her head and replied, "Not this week." And when she reached for a book, instead of telling them, "You must read this!" she turned away and placed it on the book cart without a word.

"Oh, dear," Houndsley said. But he did not have time to say more because his students were waiting for him. On Saturday mornings, Houndsley taught reading to those who didn't know how.

When Houndsley went off to teach,
Catina went to her yoga class in the big
room downstairs.

Bert waved goodbye to them both and pushed the book cart out from behind the front desk. Every Saturday morning, he helped out at the library by putting returned books back on the shelves.

The three friends went their separate ways, but each of them was thinking the same thing: *What is wrong with Trixie?*

Then, as they were leaving, they saw
the sign on the door.

This library will be closing.
Come to the party at 5:00
on Friday to say goodbye
to our beloved librarian
Trixie K. Rufflesbunny!
Please bring something
☆ special! ☆
(Final notice: All books must
be returned by Friday.)
☆

Chapter Two
Trixie

The three friends stared and blinked and read the sign three times.

"Closing?" Houndsley uttered in his soft-as-a-rose-petal voice.

"Goodbye?" Catina gasped in disbelief.

"Final!" Bert declared as tears came to his eyes.

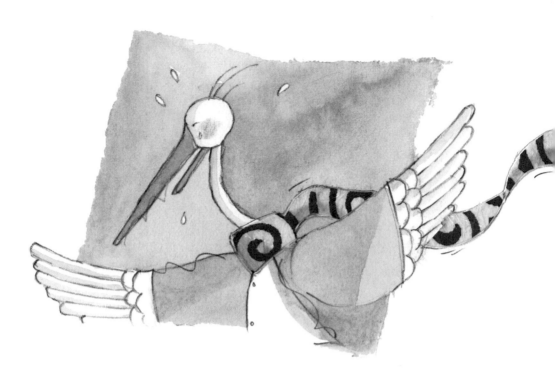

"Oh, Bert," said Houndsley. "Don't
cry. It will be all right."

"But how c-c-can it be?" Bert
sputtered. "This was our last Saturday
morning at the library. And we didn't even
know it!"

"Trixie will tell us what is going on,"
Catina said.

But Trixie could not be found.

"She left early," they were told. "She has gone home."

Houndsley, Catina, and Bert looked at one another.

"Trixie must be very sad," said Houndsley.

Catina and Bert nodded. Their friend needed them.

When they arrived at Trixie's house, she did not answer the doorbell.

"Let's look in the backyard," Houndsley suggested.

TRIXIE K.
RUFFLESBUNNY

To their surprise, there was Trixie,

jumping up and down on her trampoline.

She did not look sad at all!

As they were about to turn away,

Trixie called out, "Yoo-hoo!"

What in the world was going on?

"Let's have lemonade and I'll

explain," said Trixie.

"I was too sad to talk about it at the library," she began. "You see, I am retiring and there is no one to take my place. So the library will have to close."

"Oh, no!" Catina cried.

"That's terrible," said Bert. "How can there not be a library?"

"And why are you retiring?" asked Houndsley. "Aren't you happy being a librarian?"

"Oh, I love being a librarian, and I love reading books. And I am very sad to think of the library closing. But I have worked at the library for a long, long time.

All the books I have read have made me see that there is more I want to learn about and do. So I am going to go to circus school! It is never too late to try something new."

"Circus school sounds exciting!" said Catina.

"Very exciting!" Houndsley echoed.

Bert did not say a word. He was feeling too sad thinking that the library was going to close.

"You will come to my party, won't you?" Trixie asked.

"Of course!" they said.

As they walked away, they talked about the part of the sign that read "Please bring something special."

Bert wondered what he could bring.
What could be special enough to say thank
you to Trixie for all the happy Saturday
mornings she had given him?

Chapter Three
Something Special

All week, Houndsley carefully planned what he would bring.

Catina went in and out of the shops in town finding just the right materials for her surprise.

Meanwhile Bert paced his living room
and rearranged the books on his shelves,
thinking, *What can I bring that will be
really special?*

On Friday, the three friends gathered their library books and met at Houndsley's house. They tried being happy, but it was not easy.

"I have my something special," said Houndsley.

"So do I," said Catina. "What about you, Bert?"

Bert just shook his head. But then, as he picked up his library books and headed toward the door, he thought, *I do have something to bring!* The thought made him happy for the first time all week. Really happy.

At the library, Houndsley announced, "I have brought muffins! Pumpkin chocolate-chip, and blueberry buttermilk, and cranberry orange, and banana walnut, and cinnamon peach muffins!"

There was a loud cheer for Houndsley's muffins.

Then Catina presented Trixie with her something special.

"Oh, my!" Trixie exclaimed. "This is the most beautiful circus outfit I have ever seen! And you made it yourself! Thank you, Catina."

There was another loud cheer from the crowd.

Bert stepped forward and cleared his throat. He did not have any muffins or a fancy outfit to give Trixie. It appeared that he did not have anything at all.

"I hope you will not think I have a big head," Bert began. "The something special I brought is . . . well . . . me."

"I already think you are special," said Trixie. "You have always been such a big help here in the library."

This made Bert blush.

"It came to me when I looked at the books we were returning today," Bert went on. "I wondered what was going to happen to them once the library closed. That's when I thought of it. I know I can never replace you, Trixie, but . . .

"Well, if it would be all right . . . I would like to be the new librarian. There is a lot I don't know. But as you said, Trixie, 'It is never too late to try something new.' Would you have time to help me find a library school before you go to circus school?"

"I would love to!" Trixie cried. Everyone cheered. This cheer was even louder than the cheers that had greeted Houndsley's muffins and Catina's circus outfit.

Bert beamed.

So did Trixie. Her smile grew even bigger when she asked, "What do planets like to read?"

"I give up," Bert said. "What do planets like to read?"

"Comet books."

Everyone laughed.

Bert felt very special indeed. He had made Trixie smile and tell a joke.

"And now," Trixie said, handing Bert a book, "you must read this." The book was called *So You Want to Be a Librarian*.

"I'll start reading it tonight," said Bert.

"And tomorrow morning, I will begin to teach you everything I know," Trixie said.

Just then, someone shouted, "Look!"

The sign on the door had been changed to read:

On Saturday mornings, Houndsley and Catina and Bert go to the library just as they always have. Houndsley brings muffins for everyone.